A MIGHTY FINE TIME MACHINE

SUZANNE BLOOM

Boyds Mills Press

Honesdale, Pennsylvania

Boyds Mills Press, Inc.
815 Church Street
Honesdale, Pennsylvania 18431
Printed in the United States of America

Library of Congress Cataloging-in-Publication Data

Bloom, Suzanne.
A mighty fine time machine / Suzanne Bloom. — 1st ed.
p. cm.
Summary: An aardvark, an anteater, and an armadillo attempt to travel back in time when they
turn a big box into a time machine.
ISBN 978-1-59078-527-0 (hardcover : alk. paper)
[1. Boxes—Fiction. 2. Imagination—Fiction. 3. Play—Fiction. 4. Animals—Fiction.] I. Title.

PZ7.B6234Mi 2009
[E]—dc22
2008028043

First edition
The text of this book is set in 22-point Garamond.
The illustrations are done in gouache and colored pencil.

10 9 8 7 6 5 4 3

To my friends from the box game and the books game—
Anita, Robin, Randall, Tommy, Steven, Starr

With special thanks to
Pat McCann and Shirley the armadillo at Zoo America in Hershey, Pennsylvania,
and
Sheryl Staaden and Stella the anteater at the Jacksonville Zoo in Jacksonville, Florida

"Boys," said Sam, "you've been bamboozled."

Grant and Antoine did not know what to say.
They had just traded twenty Yummy Gummys
and a bag of Buggy Bonbons
for a time machine.

"It has no bells,
no whistles, no switches,
no horns, no knobs,
no rocket-blaster boosters,
and no thingamabobs!"
Sam pointed out.

"Believe it or not, Samantha, it's a *do-it-yourself* time machine," said Grant.

"Not only that, we have a how-to book *and* a treasure trove of hoozie-doozies," said Antoine.

Sam knew they needed her help.

They dumped everything out
and sorted through the doodads.
They plotted and planned.
They mixed and matched.

They stood back
and admired their work.
It was a mighty fine time machine,
and it was ready to launch.

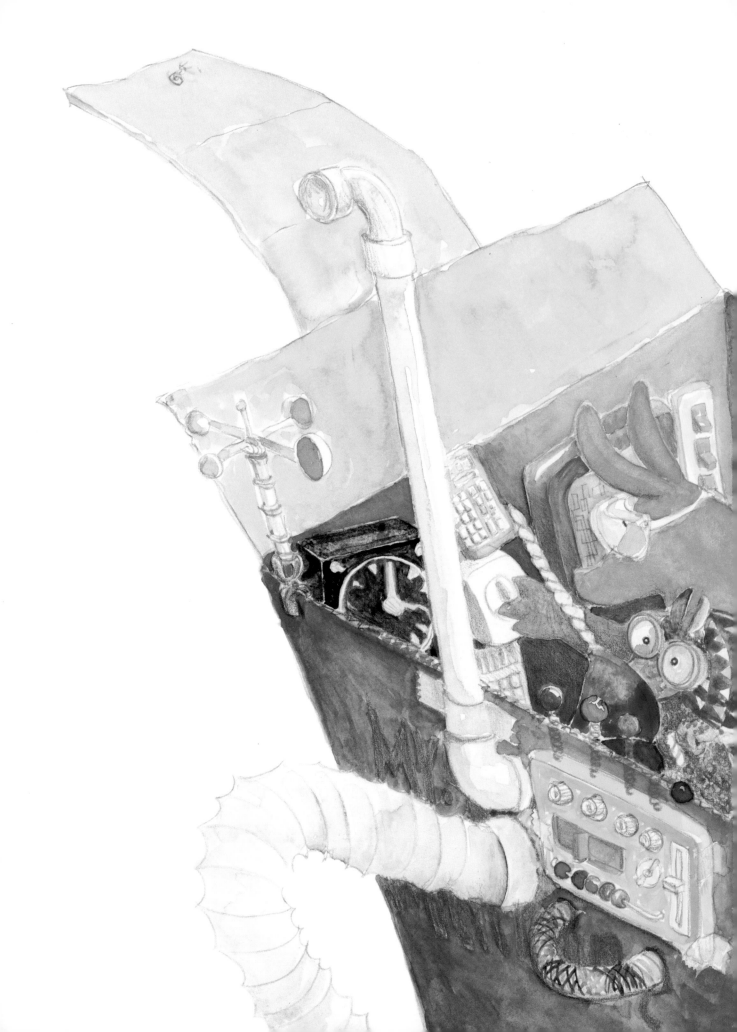

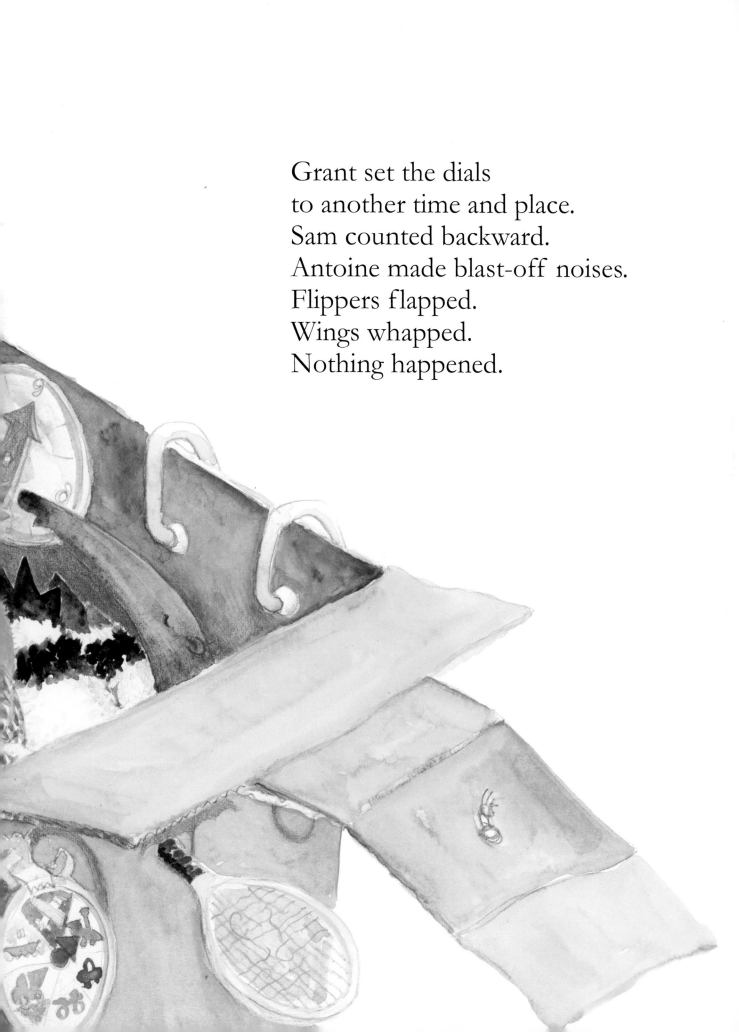

Grant set the dials
to another time and place.
Sam counted backward.
Antoine made blast-off noises.
Flippers flapped.
Wings whapped.
Nothing happened.

"We're still here," said Grant.
"It's still now," said Antoine.
"Maybe we've miscalculated," said Sam.
"Maybe it's not a rockety kind of time machine."

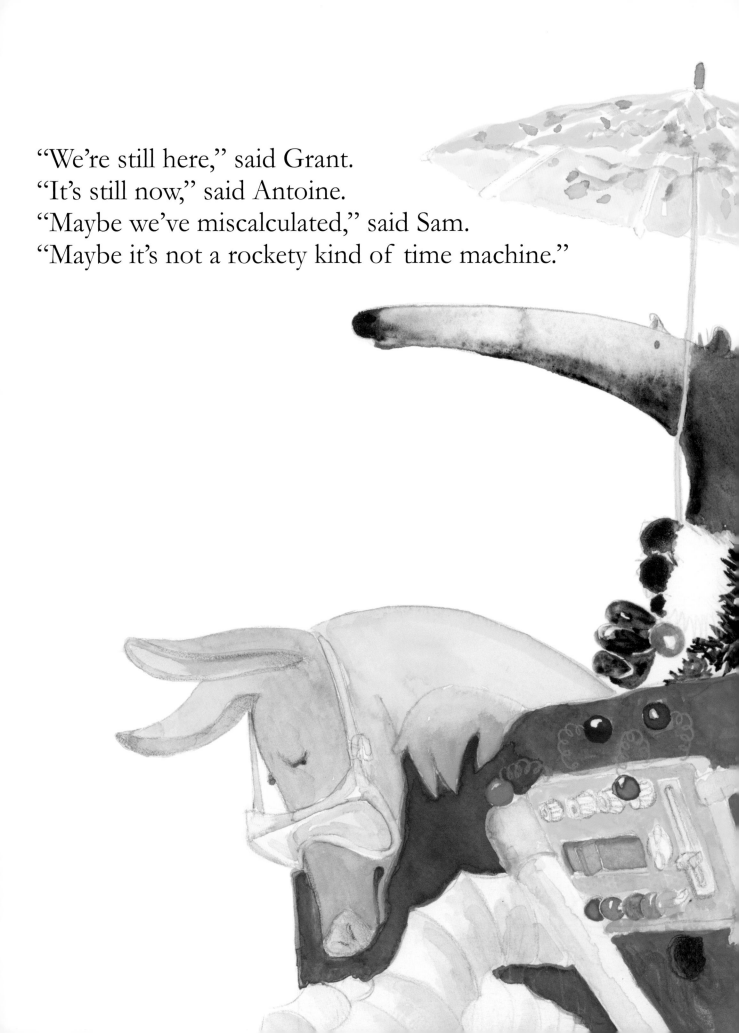

"It's rickety," said Grant.
"It's rackety," said Antoine.
But definitely not rockety, they all agreed.
"Back to work, boys."

They tinkered and tweaked
and made some minor adjustments.

They stood back to admire their work.
It was the best time machine ever,
and it was ready to roll.

Antoine spun
the wheels of time.
Samantha selected
a location on the
new map-o-meter.
Grant made
motor sounds.

It wobbled. It rocked.
It rolled down the hill.
"We did it! We did it!
We're moving!"
they cheered.

It zigzagged.
It stopped.
It toppled over.
They tumbled out
and took a look.

"It looks like we're still here," sighed Grant.
"It feels like it's still now," moaned Antoine.

"I'm hungry," said Grant.

"I'm tired," yawned Antoine.

"Don't give up now, boys," said Sam.
"Maybe we made a mistake. Maybe this isn't
a time machine after all."

Antoine said nothing.
He was tracking dinosaurs.

Grant didn't disagree.
He was flying to the moon.

Samantha went back to work. She fixed and patched.
"This is better than I thought," she said,
and made some minor adjustments.
"As a matter of fact, it's brilliant!"

She stood back to admire her work.
"Mighty fine!" she said to herself.

"Check it out, boys!"

It was the best do-it-yourself bookmobile
anyone could ever imagine!

And, believe it or not,
it worked!